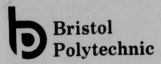

For Natasha,
with lots of love.
R. K.

For Peter and Sue,
and my son, Luke.
H. de L.

BLACKIE CHILDREN'S BOOKS
Published by the Penguin Group
Penguin Books Ltd, 27 Wrights Lane, London W8 5TZ, England
Penguin Books Australia Ltd, Ringwood, Victoria, Australia
Penguin Books Canada Ltd, 10 Alcorn Avenue, Toronto, Ontario, Canada M4V 3B2
Penguin Books (NZ) Ltd, 182 – 190 Wairau Road, Auckland 10, New Zealand

Penguin Books Ltd, Registered Offices: Harmondsworth, Middlesex, England

First published 1992
1 3 5 7 9 10 8 6 4 2

Text copyright © Rosalind Kerven, 1992
Illustrations copyright © Honey de Lacey, 1992

The moral right of the author/illustrator has been asserted

Printed in Hong Kong

A CIP catalogue record for this book is available from the British Library
ISBN 0 216 93263 7

First American edition published 1992 by
Peter Bedrick Books, 2112 Broadway, New York, NY 10023

Library of Congress Cataloging-in-Publication Data is available for this title
ISBN 0 87226 466 1

Folk Tales of the World

THE WOMAN WHO WENT TO FAIRYLAND

A Welsh Folk Tale

Retold by Rosalind Kerven
Illustrated by Honey de Lacey

Blackie
London

Bedrick/Blackie
New York

Long ago and far away over the mountains there lived an old woman and an old man called Bet and Huw. They had a farm in a quiet green valley, with no one to keep them company there except for a young serving-maid called Elin. This Elin, she was a bit of a dreamer, and a great one for daft ideas.

One bedtime, she took it into her head to leave out on the kitchen hearth a dish of bread and milk, and a big bowl of warm water with a bar of soap beside it. Well, just as she hoped, the food was all gone in the morning, the water poured away and a bright gold coin lying upon the table.

'Just look!' she cried. 'Someone came in here while we slept: they ate their supper and bathed their babies ... oh, sure to goodness, it must have been the *fairies*!'

The old couple were furious and forbade her to tempt the little
people into the house again. But Elin knew that the fields by the
river were full of their dancing rings. That night, as soon as her
work was done, she went down there to watch for them.
And very soon the fairies came to her indeed.

   They rose from the ground with the evening mist. They were
dancing, dancing - weaving and swaying into twisting lines and
circles, twirling their white robes about and tossing their long
hair. Behind them, all in step, marched the little fairy men as
well, each one of them fiddling or piping to make the strangest,
sweetest music.

As soon as they saw Elin, the fairies swept her up with them. Laughing and singing, she let them spin her round and round. The stars moved far across the sky while they danced. At last, when she was too exhausted to take another step, they lay her gently onto the dewy grass and left her there to fall fast asleep.

Old Bet had spied upon her from the farmhouse and seen everything that happened. The next day she scolded Elin: 'Listen, haven't you heard how the fairies steal away young girls they take a fancy to?'

'Such nonsense!' Elin laughed at her.

'Think what you will,' said Bet, 'but if I were you, I'd keep magic charms about me, to stop them from getting too close.'

'And what charms would they be?'

'By day,' said Bet, 'you should always carry something metal: a knife would do just nicely, one small enough to fit into your pocket. And by night you should sleep with a branch from the rowan tree lying across your bed. Metal and rowan wood: these are two things that the fairies are really afraid of, and they cannot touch you while you have them. Will you do as I advise you?'

'Maybe,' answered Elin. But she had a far away look in her eyes.

One morning old Bet and old Huw got up late. They cooked their
own breakfast and cleared away the dishes themselves, and still
there was no sign at all of Elin. So Bet went up to the little attic
bedroom where the girl slept and gave a loud knock upon the door.
When no answer came, she flung it open - and what ever do you think?
 She saw a bed that was cold and empty; and she saw the rowan branch
that was meant for protection flung carelessly into the corner on the floor.
Old Bet took one look; then she turned and went quickly downstairs again.
All the way she was shouting to Huw at the top of her voice:

'Oh what a carry-on, oh what a to-do! Lord have mercy on that foolish girl - for she's got herself stolen away by the fairies!'

A year and a day later, there was a terrible storm. Rain bucketed
down, the wind roared and lightening flashed as if the very sky
were on fire. There was a great clap of thunder, and just as it died
down they heard a loud and urgent knocking at the front door.
Old Huw went to open it. There on the step stood a fairy man!
His skin and his thick, curly hair were both as pale as moonlight.
He was no taller than a very young child.

'You'd best come in for a bit of shelter,' Huw said uncertainly.
But the fairy man shook his head at him: 'It's your wife I want.'
Bet was bustling out to see what was going on.

'Come with me,' said the fairy man as soon as he saw her.
Without waiting for an answer, he grabbed her arm and pulled
her after him, deep into the darkness of the night.

Just around the corner a silvery horse was waiting. The fairy man hoisted old Bet up on to its back, then jumped up himself behind her. The horse began to gallop through the storm. It went so fast that Bet felt as if she were flying. Shapes and shadows flashed past on either side, but she had no idea where they were going.

   Soon the horse slowed as they came to a narrow path that wound steeply up into the highest peaks. It seemed to lead to nowhere but the hard, dark rock-face. But as they reached its end, the rock gaped open and the path turned into a tunnel. In this way, the horse carried them to the innermost heart of the mountain.

The tunnel opened out into an enormous cave. It was lit by flickering oil-lamps and in one corner stood a rusty grate where a fire had burned down to glowing ashes. Such a damp and miserable place it looked, full of shadows and cobwebs. The mossy walls were all dripping and there was no sign at all of a window.

Old Bet gazed around full of wonder and horror. So *this* was Fairyland! Then she heard a gurgling cry. Upon a rough bed of dead old bracken and rushes she saw a tiny, snow-pale, newborn baby. Sitting beside it in a raggedy old dress, who should it be but Elin! The fairy man had disappeared. Bet slid down from the horse and rushed across to see her.

'Why, you poor girl!' she cried. 'Who's that little man and whatever has he done to you?'

To her surprise, she saw that Elin was laughing.

'Oh, he's the Fairy King!' said she. 'He's married me and made me his Queen. Here's our sweet little baby - and this wonderful place is our palace!'

'Oh dear, oh dear,' said Bet to herself. 'Elin must have gone soft in the head! And I suppose the fairy man has brought me here to teach her how to look after the baby.'

Well, she was a kind-hearted and capable woman. In next to no time she had heated water on the fire and was giving the little one a bath.. Afterwards, when he had had his milk, she rocked him cheerily to sleep.

But Elin insisted on putting him in the rough wooden cradle herself. Before she did so, she took a pot of ointment from a high shelf and rubbed it into the baby's eyes.

'What's that?' Bet asked her.

Elin blushed scarlet. 'It's nothing you may know about and nothing you may touch,' she said. 'It's only for the fairies. Be sure to keep well away from it, Bet, for it's mixed with the very strongest kind of magic.'

Bet was too old by far to be afraid of fairy magic. She waited and watched carefully. A few days later there came a chance when Elin was not looking. Bet reached up for the fairy ointment and rubbed a smear of it into one of her own eyes.

At once, oh marvels, what a change!

The miserable cave seemed to be transformed into a vast, magnificent palace. The floors were made of white marble and the furniture all of gold. The air smelt of flowers and echoed with light, sweet music. Beyond arched windows she glimpsed rolling meadows and sparkling waterfalls. And Elin herself was clothed now in fine trailing robes of palest gossamer with a silver crown upon her head!

Bet stared and stared and pinched herself; but still the
wonderful vision shone bright. Yet this was the strangest thing
of all: when she shut the eye with the magic ointment in it
and just looked out of the other, the gloomy cave and everything
in it appeared exactly as before.

Now Bet understood that, to those who had the magic sight, Fairyland was indeed as wonderful as Elin had dreamed. Yet she dared not talk about it, not even to Elin. Goodness knows what trouble she might get into if the fairies found out she had stolen their ointment!

'And so,' she said, 'before they find me out, I'd better be on my way home.'

She said goodbye to Elin, of course, and no sooner had she done so than the fairy man appeared again. This time Bet's magicky eye saw him in his true form, as the Fairy King: oh, so noble and handsome he looked too!

'You have given my Queen much help with our baby,' he said solemnly. 'Here is my silver horse to carry you safely home. Look, he is carrying two big packs: a gift from the Fairy People to you. But do not try to open them until you get there, or everything they contain will disappear.'

Can't you just imagine how glad old Huw was to see his wife riding home safe and sound! His mouth dropped open with astonishment when she told him everything that had happened. Then they opened the bags the King had given her and found them full to the brim with gleaming fairy gold.

Bet was so happy to be home. Yet she found it almost impossible to settle down, for a big thing bothered her. This was it: she still had the magic fairy sight in one of her eyes. Because of it, nothing at all looked as it ought to. She could see the fairies and their bits and bobs of magic gold and fancies everywhere, glittering in the cupboards, flickering through the cornfield, laughing and darting before her whenever she went for a walk. It made her feel all shivery and peculiar, but she had no idea what she could do to put things right.

Things went on uncomfortably like this until the Midwinter Fair.
Amongst the bustling stalls and sideshows there, all Bet had eyes
for were the fairies! She alone saw them come - dancing and piping
two by two. Right in the middle, riding their silvery horses, were
the King and Queen Elin themselves. Bet was so thrilled that she
pushed her way through, grabbed Elin's hand and cried: 'How are
you keeping my dear? And how's the little baby?'

Queen Elin's hand flew to her mouth and she gasped.

'Old woman,' the Fairy King said icily, 'which eye do you
see us with?'

'This one,' Bet said hoarsely. 'But please sir, I didn't ...'

The Fairy King leaned forward. Softly, he blew onto Bet's
magicky eye ...

...And in a sudden flash of light, all the fairies disappeared!

After that, old Bet never saw any sign of them again. But you can
be sure she never stopped talking about them, right to the end of
her days.